Thomas Lewis Preston

A Sketch of Mrs. Elizabeth Russell

Wife of General William Campbell, and sister of Patrick Henry

Thomas Lewis Preston

A Sketch of Mrs. Elizabeth Russell
Wife of General William Campbell, and sister of Patrick Henry

ISBN/EAN: 9783337344009

Printed in Europe, USA, Canada, Australia, Japan

Cover: Foto ©Raphael Reischuk / pixelio.de

More available books at **www.hansebooks.com**

❋ A SKETCH ❋

OF

MRS. ELIZABETH RUSSELL.

WIFE OF GENERAL WILLIAM CAMPBELL,

AND

Sister of Patrick Henry.

—

By Her Grandson,
THOMAS L. PRESTON.

NASHVILLE, TENN.:
PUBLISHING HOUSE OF THE M. E. CHURCH, SOUTH.
J. D. BARBEE, AGENT.
1888.

⇒PREFACE⇐

THIS imperfect sketch of Mrs. ELIZABETH RUSSELL was written at the request of the Rev. R. N. Price, who asked me "for a brief statement of such facts and incidents in her life as are in your possession or memory, and a word-portrait of her character." When the task was commenced the material at hand was so scanty, and the incidents in my memory so few and shadowy, that I almost despaired of producing any thing worthy of notice or a place in the "History of Holston Methodism." However, I opened a correspondence with various members of my family, and sought such scraps of information as could be gathered from tradition and fragments of old letters and other papers. To Mrs. Sallie C. P. Miller, of Princeton, New Jersey, the eldest of my nieces, I am under many obligations for valuable contributions and suggestions, as well as to other members of the family.

The investigation itself revived memories which had almost faded from my mind, and I was surprised at the distinctness with which scenes, incidents, and words were recalled. Had I not embodied the information collected, and recorded my own recollections, the incidents in Mrs. Russell's life would perhaps have been forgotten by this generation, or vaguely remembered among the traditions of the country. Most of the letters and papers of Mrs. Russell and my parents were lost by the burning of the houses in which they were stored, and many of those saved from the flames were destroyed by Federal soldiers.

The result of this "labor of love" is now submitted to the public under a deep sense of its meagerness and many imperfections, but with the hope and prayer that it may awaken in the heart of some pilgrim of earth a desire to imitate the example of this Christian woman.

THOMAS L. PRESTON.

September, 1888.

Eliz.ᵃ Russell,

P. Henry

A SKETCH

Miss ✳ Elizabeth ✳ Henry.

ELIZABETH HENRY, the daughter of John and Sarah Henry, of Hanover county, Virginia, was born July 10. 1749. She first married William Campbell, of Fincastle county, Virginia, April 2, 1776, and the following winter went with her husband to Aspenvale (now the property of Capt. Charles H. C. Preston, Smyth county, Va.), where Capt. Campbell had settled with his mother and sister in 1768. This tract of land he inherited from his father, Charles Campbell, and was a part of a royal grant of one hundred and fifty thousand acres to James Patton. By him she had two children: the elder (Sarah Buchanan), born April 21, 1778, married Gen. Francis Preston, of Montgomery county, Virginia, January 10, 1793; and the younger (Charles Henry), born Feb. 8, 1780, died Oct. 13, 1785.

Gen. William Campbell died in Hanover county, Virginia, at the house of Col. John Symms, the half-brother of his wife, Aug. 22, 1781. Mrs. Campbell afterward married Gen. Wm. Russell. By him she had four children. The eldest (Henry Winston), born 1784, died in infancy; the second (Elizabeth Henry), born in 1786, married Capt. Francis Smith, of Abingdon. Jan. 10, 1804, and died the following

October. The two youngest, Patrick and Jane, were twins, and were born in 1788. The former died when a few weeks old, and the latter married Dr. Wm. P. Thompson, of Washington county, Va.

After her marriage with Gen. Russell, they remained at Aspenvale until February, 1788, when they removed to the Salt-works in Smyth county, where Mrs. Russell continued to reside until about 1812. Gen. Russell died Jan. 14, 1793. After leaving the Salt-works, Mrs. Russell moved to a house that stood not far from the western bank of the creek above the "Town House," at that time owned and occupied by her son-in-law, Dr. Wm. P. Thompson; and this continued to be her earthly home until her death on the 18th of March, 1825.

This is an epitome of the family and life of a conspicuous woman.

Of her girlhood nothing is known. She was in Williamsburg in September, 1775, with her brother, Patrick Henry (then a widower), and sister, Mrs. Ann Christian, when Capt. William Campbell reached there with his volunteer company of riflemen, raised to aid Patrick Henry in the first organized armed movement in Virginia against the civil government of Great Britain. This movement was provoked by Lord Dunmore, who, on the 20th of April, 1775, ordered Capt. Henry Collins, of the schooner "Magdalen," at anchor in James River, to remove at night the powder in the old magazine of Williamsburg on board the "Magdalen." The restoration of it was respectfully demanded by the mayor, aldermen, and citizens, but refused by Lord Dunmore. This act of Lord Dunmore kindled like a torch the smoldering feeling of rebellion in Virginia, and in less than eight days about seven hundred "minute men," armed and equipped, assembled at Fredericksburg, ready to march to Williamsburg and demand from Lord Dunmore a restoration of the powder, and a satisfactory guarantee of its future safety for the use of the Colony. The march of these patriots was arrested by the cautious counsels of Gen. Washington, Edmund Pendleton, and others, who advised them to await the action of Congress; and by a letter from Peyton Randolph, dated April 29, 1775, in which he said that the gentlemen of the city of Williamsburg and neighborhood had full assurance from Lord Dunmore that the affair of the powder should be accommodated.

Patrick Henry, however, whose political prescience looks almost like inspiration, was not deceived by Lord Dunmore's promise; nor were his opinions modified by the weight of such authority as Washington, Pendleton, Peyton Randolph, and others. He saw the necessity of prompt action, and therefore sent express riders to notify the officers and men of the independent company of Hanover county to meet him on the 2d of May at Newcastle, on the Pamunky. Such was the effect of the address he then delivered to them that Samuel Meredith, who was captain of the company, resigned; and Henry was elected in his place. The former accepted the position of lieutenant, and Parke Goodall was appointed ensign. Under this organization the company started for Williamsburg. Messengers were sent to stop him, but Henry would not listen to temporizing counsel nor brook delay. On reaching Doncastle's Ordinary, sixteen miles from Williamsburg, he was met by Richard Corbin, his majesty's receiver-general, who was sent by Lord Dunmore to tender him a bill of exchange for £330 as "compensation for the gunpowder lately taken out of the magazine by the Governor's order." Mr. Henry accepted it, and gave Mr. Corbin a receipt, dated Doncastle's Ordinary, New Kent, May 4, 1775. (Wirt's Life of Patrick Henry, page 142.)

William Campbell was a "minute man," technically and literally, and was watching "the signs of the times." He had, with his volunteer company of riflemen, accompanied Col. Christian to Point Pleasant. Unfortunately, they reached there the night after the battle, Oct. 10, 1774. There he met Gen. Andrew Lewis, and his company was a part of those troops under Gen. Lewis who, on the 5th of

November, 1774, declared: "As the love of liberty and attachment to the real interests and just rights of America outweigh every other consideration, we resolve that we will exert every power within us for the defense of American liberty, and for the support of her just rights and privileges." And on the 20th of January, 1775 (two months afterward), he, with Cols. William Preston, Christian, Arthur Campbell, William Edmondson, and the Rev. Charles Cummings, and other leading men of Fincastle county, composing the Holston settlement, sent a calm and patriotic address to the Continental Congress, announcing that "if no specific measures shall be proposed and adopted by Great Britain, and our enemies attempt to dragoon us out of those inestimable privileges which we are entitled to as subjects, and reduce us to slavery, we declare that we are deliberately and resolutely determined never to surrender them to any power upon earth, but at the expense of our lives. These are our real, though unpolished, sentiments of liberty and loyalty, and in them we are resolved to live and die." ("King's Mountain and Its Heroes," page 381: American Archives, Fourth Series, I. 993–1168.) Influenced by these antecedents, Capt. Campbell was on the alert, waiting for developments from the east. As soon, therefore, as the echoes of Patrick Henry's voice reverberated among the hills of the Holston valley, he called his company of riflemen together—those terrible "shirt men"—and marched to Williamsburg, a distance of more than four hundred miles, before the autumn leaves fell upon their pathway. Such promptness and zealous patriotism were eloquence in action, and secured for the gallant mountaineer a cordial welcome into the family circle of Patrick Henry.

Capt. Campbell was of superb *physique*, six feet two inches high, straight, and soldierly in his bearing, quiet and polished in manners, and always deferential and chivalric toward women. His complexion was fair and fresh, without being ruddy, and his eyes were light blue and full, though not prominent, and varied in expression with every emotion. His brow was smooth and full, and his hair light brown with a tinge of red. In repose, his mouth and chin, which were finely shaped, expressed decision of character; and when his countenance lighted up with pleasure or affection, the smile was as soft and sweet as a woman's. But when roused to anger, there were few who did not quail under the concentrated gaze of those brilliant eyes.

The first meeting of Miss Elizabeth Henry and Capt. Campbell was under circumstances well calculated to make a most favorable impression on each. These first impressions soon deepened into warmer feelings, and they were married the ensuing spring.

The military duties of Capt. Campbell kept him in Williamsburg, or where the services of his company were required, until the winter of 1776, when he returned with his wife to Aspenvale. He was at Abingdon on the 1st of January, 1777, and aided in the organization of Washington county. (Howe's History of Virginia, page 501.)

From an early period of their married life, Mrs. Campbell exercised a softening and admirable influence upon her husband. The best exposition of his high regard and tender love for her is the following letter. It is written in a very clear, round hand, as distinct as a copy-plate. The paper now looks rough and flimsy, but must have been originally smooth and firm to receive such delicate strokes of this beautiful penmanship. The dimensions of the sheet are unusual for these times, being sixteen and a quarter inches long by ten inches wide; yet across these ten inches the lines are nearly as straight and regular as though they were ruled, and there are no erasures, and very few interlineations:

WILLIAMSBURG, August 18, 1776.

My Dearest Betsy: When I wrote you last it was in the greatest hurry, and had only time to inform you that I was permitted to continue at this place until the time for which I engaged expires. I thought to have wrote to you by John Henry, but he went off unknown to me; since, I have had no opportunity only by post, and I now write without knowing of a conveyance.

Last Tuesday a man (Sam Newell) arrived here by express in five days from my house, by whom I was informed that a fort is built there, and that about four hundred people, consisting of men, women, and children, have collected to it. This has removed much of my anxiety, as I hope my mother and sisters will be prudent enough not to expose themselves to danger, and the men gathered there will be a means of preserving the crop at least.

Eighteen of our men, two or three women, and some children, have been killed. Our people have scalped twenty-seven Indians, and it is thought that many more have been killed, from the large quantities of blood that flowed from those who were wounded and ran away. Three Indians were seen about half a mile from my house, and several small parties have been discovered a considerable way on this side. I have now the scalp of one who was killed eight or nine miles from my house about three weeks ago. The first time I go up I shall take it along to let you see it. From the success our people have hitherto had in every encounter with the Indians I flatter myself that these savages are much intimidated, and that they are now convinced they cannot make such an easy conquest as they at first imagined.

I received your sweet and most affectionate letter of the 9th inst. by Col. Meredith. The fear you there express for my going to the northward, or against the Cherokees, you may entirely lay aside. My fate has done you this favor, I must confess, even against my inclination. I last week applied to the General for leave to go home, and was peremptorily refused. He ordered me to stay here, and take command of the soldiers belonging to the first regiment who continue at this place. I do not yet know how long I will be obliged to stay here. I make no doubt but it will be above a month yet. If the horse you mentioned please you right well, by all means buy him; though inquire . . . the . . . if he is given either to stumbling or starting; they are . . . especially in a woman's hackney.

I most heartily thank you, my dear, for your attention, for providing me such necessaries as I stand in need of. I fear you are too solicitous and give yourself too much trouble. You bring to my mind Solomon's excellent description of a good wife: "She seeketh wool, and flax, and worketh willingly with her hands. She layeth her hands to the spindle, and her hands hold the distaff. She maketh herself coverings of tapestry; her clothing is silk and purple. Her husband is known in the gates, when he sitteth among the elders of the land." Such is my dearest Betsy. Her worth I esteem far above rubies.

I have now lived about a week in the house where I was first blessed with a sight of my dear Betsy. Little did I at that time think that such superlative happiness was destined for me. From that happy moment I date the hour of all my bliss. I love the place on your account.

It is uncertain when I shall have the happiness of seeing you again, as I seem to be more than ever confined. I have the charge of about two hundred men, at least one-third of them sick, and but two subalterns in the whole who are able to do duty, and they are at this time upon a command at Jamestown; so that I have not just now an officer in camp to assist me in the least. This will always be the case unless we are incorporated with some other regiment, which I do not know whether the General designs or not.

I have got the needles and pins for you which you wrote for. I wish they may answer the purpose, as I believe both are the manufacture of Philadelphia, and the first attempts in things of that kind do not in common succeed very well. No such thing as a card to be procured here. Had you not better get several pairs of the clothier's cards, which I heard you talk of? They will be better than none at all. If you can get a good many pairs of them, as their price is trifling, you might . . . taken by the girls about you; though you are the best judge of this yourself.

By Sam Newell I wrote to Col. Christian, and hinted to him that I was desirous to have soldiers stationed at my place, if he thought there was any necessity for them there. It will be the means of preventing the people from flying farther off if they could think themselves safe there. Newell could not inform me whether the Colonel would accept of the command upon the expedition, as the letters from the Council had not come to his hands when Newell came along.

I have been tolerably well since I came down, but do not recover my health near so fast as while I was with you. I most heartily wish my . . . this country; it does not at all agree with our highland constitutions. . . . Will see you as soon as I possibly can.

May you be the peculiar . . . heaven, and that you may enjoy every necessary blessing and comfort, . . . dearest Betsy. Your most affectionate
WM. CAMPBELL.

P. S.—Our friend Mr. Trigg is recovering fast. He is now able to take an airing in a chair, and has walked this day from Captain Anderson's to pay me a visit. He thanks you for the apples you sent him, and acknowledges them as a very grateful present. W. C.

To her he was always gentle, considerate, and affectionate. When provoked to anger, a look or word from her relaxed the knit brow and lighted his expressive face with a sweet, bright smile.

His hatred of Tories was a passion. He had learned something of their character in Eastern Virginia. At his own home they had badgered him by every means of annoyance. Upon his gate-posts they had fastened placards threatening his life, and he knew he was watched and waylaid.

The only hope of peace and safety for his family and himself, as well as for that of the community, was to drive these traitors from the country and extinguish by every means this element of discord and danger. Among them there were some persons of "doubtful minds;" and while they secretly aided and abetted the Tories, they tried to preserve a fair standing with the patriots. Such a one lived not far from Aspenvale, and, dreading Col. Campbell's wrath, he came one day to his house when he knew he was absent, to beg Mrs. Campbell to intercede for him. During the interview, and while most humbly beseeching her to interpose in his behalf, the front door was opened, and in walked the Colonel. A glance at his face made the Tory spring from his seat and rush for the backdoor. The Colonel whipped out his sword, and was in the act of bringing it down with all the power of his strong arm upon the Tory's head, when Mrs. Campbell sprung forward and caught his upraised elbow. This made the point of the sword strike the lintel of the door, and saved the Tory's head. So powerful was the blow that it cut a deep gash in the hard oak lintel and bent the point of that celebrated "Andrea de Ferrara." The bend could never be entirely straightened, and there it remains to this day.* As soon as the paroxysm of passion was over, Gen. Campbell turned to his wife, and, moved by the expression of her face, caught her in his arms and thanked her for saving the life of the poor fellow, who, though he deserved to be hanged, ought not to be cut down under his roof and in her presence.

The execution of Francis Hopkins, the notorious Tory and desperado, in the summer of 1779, is an historical incident of such importance that it should not be omitted in any

---

* Mrs. Preston, daughter of Gen. Wm. Campbell, kept this sword on brackets fastened to the wall at the head of her bed, and when drawn from its scabbard to be cleaned and oiled, the bend at the point was shown to her children as a memento of this incident. Gen. John S. Preston wore this sword in the war between the States, and it is now the property of his grandson, Wm. C. Preston.

notice of the life of either Gen. Campbell or his wife. It was characteristic of the times, and gives an insight into the state of society and sentiment of the period. It has been widely circulated, often repeated, and generally misrepresented, because the facts were not accurately known. The account given by Mr. Lyman C. Draper, in "King's Mountain and Its Heroes," pages 384–387, is the fullest, and, except in a few immaterial circumstances and the omission of some facts, accurate in all its details. My version of the story was obtained chiefly from my mother, Mrs. Sarah B. Preston, daughter of Gen. Wm. Campbell, who heard it, doubtless, from those who were actors in it; and from old John Brawdy, the faithful body-servant of Gen. Campbell.

To appreciate properly the conduct of those who were most prominent in this transaction, their relative positions should be kept distinctly before the mind, as well as the period at which it occurred.

Col. Campbell was a magistrate, as well as military commandant of that district of Washington county, and exercised both civil and military authority, and in this twofold capacity was, in a great measure, responsible for the good order and safety of the citizens within his district.

Francis Hopkins was an outlaw and a desperate Tory—a terror to the unprotected families of the neighborhood. He had been convicted of passing counterfeit money, and imprisoned at Cocke's Fort on Renfroe's Creek. His confederates in crime at night pried the prison-door from its hinges and delivered him. He took refuge with the openly armed enemies of the State in North Carolina, and from them accepted "a commission with letters to the Cherokee Indians and the white emissaries among them, urging them to fall upon the frontier settlers with fagot, knife, and tomahawk." ("King's Mountain and Its Heroes.") He was at that time on his way to meet them, and doubtless expected to enlist recruits and obtain horses in that portion of Virginia for his nefarious expedition. In short, he was an enemy of mankind, and, like Cain, deserved death at the hands of every man.   It was in the summer of 1779, just after the daring and dangerous uprising of Tories in Montgomery county, Va., had been suppressed by the promptness and energy of Col. Walter Crockett.   The public mind was much excited, and a restless feeling of insecurity pervaded all that portion of the State.

The account given of the "start" in the race after Hopkins was often told me by John Brawdy, the body-servant of Col. Wm. Campbell; and his statements were corroborated by Mrs. Sarah B. Preston, Col. Campbell's daughter. It was briefly this:

" One bright Sunday evening we—massa and missus, and many of de neighbors—were coming home from de Ebbny Spring church, whar we had been to preaching, and as we were riding along slowly up de hill about half a mile or so below de Stone House,* and just as dem in front got to de top, dey all stopped right still in de road.   I was behind, when Massa Billy (de Colonel, you know) turned round and called me, and said, 'Come here quickly, John.' I whipped up my horse and came along close up to his side, for I knowed when he spoke dat way he was in a hurry, and I had to be lively in my motions.   As soon as I got in reach, he handed me de baby he was toting on a piller before him, and said, 'Take care of her and your missus, John;' and I hardly got her in my arms before he dug de spurs in his horse, and hollerd, 'Follow, men!' and dey all went off like mad.   I never seed such a scampering as dar was dat day.   And dar I was left a-standing in de road wid de baby in my arms, and missus and de other ladies of de company.   And dat leetle baby dat I carried before me on de piller dat day was your own mother, my blessed young missus."

---

*The Stone House, now the property of James Byars, was the citadel of the fort at that place, built in 1776.   It is of stone, with double walls, pierced for musketry, and was covered with a thick coating of mortar to prevent its being set on fire.   It was proof against the arrows of the Indians and the small arms of the period.

Besides the group which composed Col. Wm. Campbell's party, and are mentioned by Mr. Draper in "King's Mountain and Its Heroes" (viz., John Campbell and family, Capt. Jas. Dysart and wife, James Fullen, and——Faris) there were others returning in the same direction from church; and although they did not join in the chase, they followed more leisurely to the place of capture. If I mistake not, one of these was Mr. Greaver, grandfather of Gen. Jas. S. Greaver, late Senator in the Legislature of Virginia.

As Col. Campbell's party reached the summit of the hill mentioned by John Brawdy, they saw a man approaching from the opposite direction. As soon as he observed them he turned quickly out of the road into the woods. As prompt, however, as was his action, he was recognized by John Campbell, who said to Col. Wm. Campbell, "That's Frank Hopkins." The announcement of this name startled the entire party, and all were ready for the dash as soon as Col. Campbell put his child in the arms of his servant. When he gave the command, "Follow, men!" all started at full speed. Hopkins had turned back into the road when he thought he was out of sight of the party returning from church. His pursuers, on reaching the eastern descent of the hill, saw him a few hundred yards in advance, urging his horse with whip and spur. The race was for life, and the avengers' pursuit was furious. They soon discovered they were gaining rapidly on the fugitive. He heard the clatter of the hoofs, and saw, as he glanced back, that the foremost horseman would soon be upon him if he kept to the open road. By a sudden and strong effort he wheeled his horse, and plunging the spurs into his sides made him leap from the bank into the river. The leap and the water suddenly checked the horse and threw Hopkins on the pommel of the saddle. Before he could recover his seat and urge the horse to further exertion, Col. Campbell forced his horse into the stream and was by his side. Col. Campbell threw himself into the river, and, as he did so, seized the holsters on Hopkins's saddle, and jerking them off dropped them into the water. With his other hand he caught the bridle-rein of Hopkins's horse, and, quickly drawing his sword, ordered him to surrender. Surprised by the quickness of Col. Campbell's action, Hopkins sat upon his horse dazed and motionless; and as they thus faced each other, Col. Campbell waist-deep in water, other members of the party arrived, and surrounding Hopkins escorted him to the river's bank.

A court of "oyer and terminer" was improvised, and witnesses were called and sworn "to tell the truth, the whole truth, and nothing but the truth," and upon their testimony, and other evidence then and there produced, Hopkins was convicted of crimes adjudged worthy of death. The commission and letters to the Cherokee Indians were found upon his person. The horse he rode had been stolen that day, and the halters tied to his saddle were evidently intended for others to be obtained in the same way.

After conviction, short shrift was given the culprit. He was hanged with one of his own halters to a limb of the sycamore-tree which canopied court, witnesses, and spectators, and was buried among its roots. Silently and sadly the company dispersed from this solemn and memorable scene.

When Col. Campbell rejoined his wife she eagerly inquired, "What did you do with him, Mr. Campbell?" "O we hung him, Betty—that's all!" *

At that time there were no secure jails in the country. Col. Campbell and his associates had neither leisure nor inclination for guarding and bringing to a formal trial at the court-house such a dangerous outlaw as Hopkins. They therefore executed him, not as an excited mob administering lynch law, but deliberately, as loyal citizens of Virginia, and under enlightened consciences and a full sense of their responsibility to God and their country; and the country generally approved and indorsed their conduct, as is estab-

---

* King's Mountain and Its Heroes, page 384.

lished by the fact that at the next session of the Legislature in October an act was passed, at the instance of Gen. Thomas Nelson, specifically and fully exonerating and indemnifying Col. Campbell and those who acted with him.

There are no letters nor other written evidence now existing to reveal the daily life of Col. and Mrs. Campbell. When at home, and not engaged in public duties, he aided in the cultivation of his farm, and held the plow with his own hands. One day, after he had issued a mandate requiring all the men of that district to report at his house and renew their oaths of allegiance to Virginia, he was plowing the field in front of it, when Mitchell Scott rode up. Tying his horse to the fence, he climbed over, and waited until the Colonel came around to the place where he was standing. The Colonel stopped his team, greeted Scott very kindly, then turned the plow out of the furrow and sat upon the beam, and motioned Scott to a seat by his side, prepared for a chat. They discussed the topics of the day and neighborhood, and then Scott, rising, said: " Well, Colonel, I got your notice about taking the oath of allegiance, and I have come to renew mine." The Colonel looked at him for a moment, and replied: "Why, Scott, you know I did not intend that notice for you, or for such men as you are, but for those secret Tories and half-hearted patriots. We must find out who these are, and make them do their duty or rid the country of them." Scott was an Irishman, a true patriot, and a man of courage. He was quick to take a hint, and prompt to act upon it. An incident in Mr. Scott's life illustrates his character. His house was not far from the Salt-works valley, and the path leading to it passed through a dense canebrake. On one occasion he was going along this path with a spade upon his shoulder, and in the narrowest part of it and thickest growth of cane a fine snag buck, bloody and furious from a recent fight, confronted him. As soon as the animal saw Scott he turned his hair the wrong way and rushed at him. Scott grasped the spade with both hands and braced himself for the attack.

and just as the buck lowered his head for the fatal lunge struck him between the horns and cleft the skull down to the eyes.

Mrs. Campbell was doubtless occupied by the routine duties incident to a frontier life and an isolated position. Her influence, however, extended beyond the home circle; and it was that influence which made the house of Col. Campbell the most attractive in all that country. He won the esteem and confidence of the men, molded their opinions, and inspired them with his own high principles and zealous patriotism. They looked up to him as their leader, and loved, trusted, and obeyed him. Hence the facility with which he assembled and organized the volunteer companies in the autumns of 1774 and 1775, and that noble and gallant regiment which he led to and commanded at King's Mountain in 1780.

To Mrs. Campbell came the poor and the distressed as to one from whom they were sure of relief and sympathy and wise counsel, while the better classes were attracted by her social qualities and the charm of her manners and conversation. During his frequent absences on civil and military duty, she needed no other protection than that of their faithful slaves and the kind neighbors, who regarded her as a sacred charge to be looked after and guarded with zealous care. She was, however, a woman of great courage and self-reliance, and habitually, in prayer, committed her safekeeping to God, who watched over and spared her for other and greater work in the years to come.

Col. Campbell was a member of the Legislature in 1780, and on the 14th of June was elected a brigadier-general of militia to serve under the Marquis de Lafayette, then commanding in Virginia. On the 16th he obtained leave of absence for the remainder of the session, and reported at once for service to Gen. Lafayette, who assigned him to the command of a brigade of light infantry and riflemen. At that time Cornwallis was encamped at Williamsburg, and Gen. Lafayette's army six miles distant on the road to Richmond. While engaged in active service General Campbell was taken with an acute disease of the chest or bowels. He was carried to Col. John Symm's (Mrs. Campbell's half-brother), in Hanover county, where, after a few days' illness, he died on the 22d of August, 1781. The blow to his wife was unexpected and overwhelming. When the news of his death reached the Holston valley, a deep gloom settled upon the community, and they mourned as for a national calamity. Nor did this feeling soon pass away. In after years, when the white wings of peace had spread over the country, it was manifested by his friends and comrades-in-arms, who would come to his house, take his little daughter—his only surviving child—upon their knees, pet and caress her, talk to her about her father, and tell of his gallant and chivalric deeds in war, and of his kindness and generosity, until the tears streamed down their cheeks. These stories, told with such graphic simplicity and touching pathos by the veterans of the Revolution, made a deep and lasting impression upon the child, and filled her mind with an ideal hero for whom, during all her life, she cherished a reverence and love that bordered on adoration.

During Mrs. Campbell's widowhood she resided at Aspenvale. Gen. William Russell came to that neighborhood, where he owned a tract of land, in 1781. He became acquainted with Mrs. Campbell, and interested himself in her business affairs. He obtained patents for the bounty lands given by the State of Virginia to Col. Wm. Campbell and Lieut. Samuel Campbell, and located the patent for 2,666⅔ acres belonging to the heirs of Lieut. Campbell, with his own patents on Caldwell's Creek, a branch of Green River, in Kentucky. He and Mrs. Campbell were married in 1783.

Gen. Wm. Russell was tall and of commanding presence, soldierly in his bearing, courteous in manner, and refined and cultivated in conversation. But underneath this smooth and polished exterior there was a proud, stern nature and an imperious temper. The discipline in his family was austere, and so harshly did it press upon his step-daughter, Sarah B. Campbell, that her uncle Arthur Campbell applied to the court of Washington county to have her taken from his guardianship. This was done in 1789; and Capt. Thomas Madison, her uncle-in-law, being appointed her

guardian, removed her to the affectionate and congenial
influences of his family circle.

After their marriage in 1783, Gen. and Mrs. Russell
lived an uneventful life at Aspenvale until February, 1788,
when they moved to the Salt-works—then called the "Salt
Lick"—in Smyth county, and afterward known as "Preston's Salt-works." This they did in order that Gen. Russell
might give his personal attention to the manufacture of
salt, which was rapidly developing into an important in-
dustry.

It was in the ensuing month of April that both of them
were converted to Methodism, of which the Rev. Thomas
Ware, in his "Life," gives the following account:

Our first Conference in Holston was held in May, 1788. As the road by
which Bishop Asbury was to come was infested with hostile savages, so that
it could not be traveled except by considerable companies together, he was
detained for a week after the time appointed to commence. But we were
not idle, and the Lord gave us many souls in the place where we were assembled; among them were Gen. Russell and lady, the latter a sister of the
illustrious Patrick Henry. I mention these particularly, because they were
the first-fruits of our labors at this Conference.

On the Sabbath we had a crowded audience, and Mr. Tunnell preached an
excellent sermon, which produced great effect. The sermon was followed by
a number of powerful exhortations. When the meeting closed, Mrs. Russell came to me and said: 'I thought I was a Christian; but, sir, I am not a
Christian—I am the veriest sinner upon earth. I want you and Mr. Mastin
to come with Mr. Tunnell to our house and pray for us, and tell us what we
must do to be saved.' So we went, and spent much of the afternoon in prayer,
especially for Mrs. Russell; but she did not obtain deliverance. Being much
exhausted, the preachers retired to a pleasant grove near at hand to spend a
short time.

After we retired, the General, seeing the agony of soul under which his
poor wife was laboring, read to her, by the advice of his pious daughter, Mr.
Fletcher's charming address to mourners, as contained in his 'Appeal.' At
length we heard the word 'Glory!' often repeated, accompanied with the
clapping of hands. We hastened to the house, and found Mrs. Russell
praising the Lord, and the General walking the floor and weeping bitterly,
uttering at this time this plaintive appeal to the Saviour of sinners: 'O Lord,
thou didst bless my dear wife while thy poor servant was reading to her; hast
thou not also a blessing for me?' At length he sat down quite exhausted.
This scene was in a high degree interesting to us. To see the old soldier and

statesman, the proud opposer of godliness, trembling, and earnestly inquiring what he must do to be saved, was an affecting sight. But the work ended not here. The conversion of Mrs. Russell, whose zeal, good sense, and amiableness of character were proverbial, together with the penitential grief so conspicuous in the General, made a deep impression upon the minds of many, and many were brought in before the Conference closed. The General rested not until he knew his adoption; and he continued a faithful member of the Church, and an official member after he became eligible to office, constantly adorning the doctrine of God our Saviour until the end of his life.

Under deep conviction and spiritual excitement, Mrs. Russell said: "I thought I was a Christian; but, sir, I am not a Christian—I am the veriest sinner upon earth." And yet Mr. Ware states that "her zeal, good sense, and amiableness of character were proverbial." These traits of character bear testimony not only to the influence of early training and natural disposition, but also to a life governed by the principles of the Christian religion. Her father, John Henry, was a member of the Episcopal Church, and the lives of his children illustrated the abiding influence of parental piety. Patrick Henry was one of the purest and most exemplary men of the Revolution. He was an habitual reader of the Bible, and accepted it as a revelation from God; and although he never united himself to any Church, his spotless moral character was evidence of a firm belief and trusting faith in Jesus. He neither swore nor gambled nor drank, and there was a gentleness and child-like simplicity in his intercourse with his friends, but more especially in his family, that resembled, if it were not, the genuine fruit of God's Spirit upon the human heart.

The impression made by Mrs. Russell on her acquaintances and friends, previous to her avowed conversion, was that she was a Christian. She may have quieted her conscience by a formal observance of external ceremonies, and lulled it by a dangerous confidence in and reliance upon a pure, spotless morality. From this fatal self-delusion, known only to God, her soul was aroused by the fervent preaching and exhortations of Messrs. Tunnell, Ware, and others. Awakened to the true spiritual condition of her soul, she faltered not, but "in agony of tears" prayed for pardon and peace. Like the wind the Spirit came, and, wafting away the clouds which darkened, let the light of God's reconciled countenance shine upon her heart. From that moment she consecrated herself to God, and her subsequent life was in absolute harmony with the professions then made. Not many days after her conversion Bishop Asbury arrived, and in his Journal made the following entry:

1788, Virginia. Saturday, 31 (May). We came to Gen. Russell's—a most kind family indeed and in truth.

Sunday, 4.—Preached on Phil. ii. 5–9. I found it good to get alone in prayer.

The significance of the last sentence is made apparent by a glance at the privations and hardships he had undergone in the fatiguing journey from Rutherford Court-house, in North Carolina, to the comfortable house of a refined family. His pathway had been through primitive forests and over rough and lofty mountains. The country was sparsely settled, and it was difficult to obtain shelter in the rough log-cabins on the way, and food for man or beast. The guests and family occupied the same room, and there was no privacy and no opportunity for meditation or prayer. To the Bishop, sick and suffering, this was a sad privation, and one of the sore trials in his laborious episcopal and apostolic work.

The first Holston Conference was held at Halfacre's and Keywood's, about three miles from Gen. Russell's. The Bishop says: "The weather was cold, the room without fire, and otherwise uncomfortable; we nevertheless made out to keep our seats until we had finished the essential part of our business."

In this immediate neighborhood was soon afterward built Mahanaim Church, of substantial hewed logs; and there it stood until some few years ago, when "decay's effacing fingers" made it unsafe, and it was pulled down, and a substantial frame building erected upon its site.

Again, in 1790, Bishop Asbury visited this part of Virginia, and on April 20th enters in his Journal: "We had a good prayer-meeting at Gen. Russell's. This family is lavish in attention and kindness. I was nursed as an only child by the good man and woman of the house, and indeed by all the family. God Almighty bless them and reward them!"

In May, 1793, the Bishop says:

Saturday, 19.—Came to Sister Russell's. I am very solemn. I feel the want of the dear man who, I trust, is now in Abraham's bosom, and hope erelong to see him there. He was a general officer in the Continental army, where he underwent great fatigue. He was powerfully brought to God, and for a few years past was a living flame and a blessing to his neighborhood. He went in the dead of winter on a visit to his friends, was seized with an influenza, and ended his life from home. O that the gospel may continue in this house!

The Bishop did not fail to visit Mrs. Russell in after years when his episcopal duties required him to pass through that portion of the State, and these he chronicles in his Journal in 1797, 1801, and 1802. Mrs. Russell regarded them as "times of refreshing from the Lord," anticipated them with pleasure, and referred to them as bright epochs in her life.

In 1792 Gen. Russell's health failed. He decided, however, to attend the Legislature—of which he was a member —that winter in Richmond, and to pay his son Robert S. Russell, who lived in Shenandoah county, a visit on the way. But before leaving home he became so feeble and apprehensive about his condition that his wife, with their two youngest daughters, and his son-in-law—the Rev. Hubbard Saunders—with his wife, decided to accompany him. They left home on the 15th day of December, 1792, and did not reach Robert S. Russell's until the 1st of January, 1793. On the way the party stopped and rested at Capt. Thos. Madison's (guardian of Mrs. Russell's daughter, Miss Sarah B. Campbell), in Botetourt county. After reaching his son's, Gen. Russell, who had taken a bad cold on the journey, grew rapidly worse, and died on the 14th.

Soon after that sad journey and its sadder termination,

Mrs. Russell returned to her home at the Salt-works. The family circle was in a little while broken up. Gen. Russell's children by his first marriage went to their own homes in Kentucky, and the widow was left with her two little daughters, Elizabeth and Jane, the former seven and the latter five years old.

On the 6th of May, 1793, she was appointed administratrix of her husband's estate; but after two years she made a settlement, and resigned this responsible position on the 28th of April, 1795.

Not long afterward she entered into an agreement with Gen. Russell's children, by which she relinquished to them her entire right of dower in all his real estate for little more than a nominal consideration, but stipulated that the relinquishment should not affect the interests of her daughters Elizabeth and Jane.

About the same time she manumitted absolutely all the slaves she owned in fee-simple, and those she held by right of dower were set free during her life. These latter, and notably among them John Brawdy, were provided with homes on the Salt-works estate—which had been much enlarged by the entry or purchase of adjoining lands—where they lived until her death in 1825.

John Brawdy held a free lease for life on a rich tract of land on the river above the Salt-works, where he raised a large family, and lived respected by white and colored until about 1848. In his old age, when asked how old he was, he would reply: " Well, master, I really don't know exactly; but I reckon I must be more than a hundred—I done see so much." He was about ninety-five, or perhaps one hundred.

It is a striking fact, and worthy of mention in this connection, that not one of the dower negroes attempted to escape during the period of their temporary freedom. On the death of Mrs. Russell they were incorporated among the slaves of Gen. Francis Preston, and some of them were made house and body servants and distributed among his children. So identified with and faithful to the family

SALT-WORKS VALLEY AND RESIDENCE OF GENERAL FRANCIS PRESTON.

were they that they became the trusted servants of those to whom they were given, and were true to them in South Carolina, Louisiana, Mississippi, and Virginia, during and since the civil war. One branch of the family belonged to the writer, and is now the trusted head man of his household, and is the fifth "Kiah" in regular descent from the slave who belonged to Mrs. Elizabeth Russell.

Mrs. Russell also gave up her dower interest in General Campbell's estate to her daughter, Mrs. Sarah B. Preston.

By these acts of self-abnegation and generosity she was disentangling herself from the responsibilities and cares of the world, and preparing to dedicate her time and thoughts to the greater interests of eternity.

Gen. Francis Preston married Sarah B. Campbell on the 10th of January, 1793, at Capt. Thomas Madison's; went soon afterward to Washington county, and that same year was elected to Congress. It then met in Philadelphia, whither he went with his young and beautiful wife. There, on the 27th of December, 1794, William C. Preston was born, on South Fourth street, opposite the African church.

On the adjournment of Congress he came to and fixed his home at the Salt-works. The house he occupied had been built by Capt. Thomas Madison, and was on the south side of the valley, immediately opposite to that of Mrs. Russell at the base of the northern hills. At that time nearly one-third of the valley was covered with water, and between Mrs. Russell's and Gen. Preston's there was an open pond, or lake, more than a quarter of a mile wide, and quite half a mile long. In winter, large flocks of wild ducks, geese, and swan frequented it. One of the old settlers told me, and often recurred to the fact, that his mother gave him a pint of cream for every swan he would kill, and would add, "I got my cream nearly every day."

Canoes and skiffs were put upon the pond and used by hunters to shoot from, and recover this game. On damp nights the will-with-a-wisp, or jack-with-a-lantern, was often seen flitting among the tall flags and weeds that grew near the margin of the lake. This flickering and mysterious light was a fruitful source of superstition, and was the foundation of many weird witch stories among the simple and imaginative whites and credulous negroes.

The distance in an air line from Mrs. Russell's to Gen. Preston's is about eleven hundred yards; and so remarkable were the vision and the voice of the former that she could distinguish the members of the family in the porch or yard at Gen. Preston's, and would call to them and ask how they were. The reply was given by concerted signals, for no other voice sent articulate sentences across that level expanse.

Mrs. Russell's daughter Elizabeth married Capt. Francis Smith—a first cousin of Gen. Preston, and then an inmate of his family—January 10th, 1804. Not long after the marriage her health gave way, and she died the following October. At the time of her death the agonizing screams of the bereaved mother were distinctly heard by the family at Gen. Preston's.

Mrs. Smith was buried, at her own request, on the summit of the "Sugar Loaf," a conical hill west of and near Gen. Preston's, at the western base of which issues the spring which supplies the water for driving a twenty-foot mill-wheel not more than fifty yards distant. From the "Sugar Loaf" there is a charming view of the valley and surrounding country, of Mrs. Russell's house, and the white and red rocks which crown the crest of Clinch Mountain. It is one of the most beautiful and picturesque landscapes of Virginia. Mrs. Smith's remains were removed to the family burying-place at Aspenvale in 1842. After thirty-eight years of sepulture, the rich auburn hair retained much of its freshness, and coiled in massive folds where the head of that lovely young woman had been laid to rest.

When Gen. Preston and his family moved to Abingdon, in 1812, Mrs. Russell decided to leave the Salt-works. In the meanwhile her youngest daughter, Jane, had married Dr. William Patton Thompson, who lived at the "Town

House," now the property of Mr. C. Beattie. It was so called because from its roof, as was supposed, Abingdon could be seen, a distance of eighteen miles.

Dr. Thompson's landed estate was one of the largest and finest in all that section of country. It extended from Aspenvale on the east to below Gen. Greavor's on the west, and from the Chestnut Ridge on the south to Walker's Mountain on the north, and embraced eight or ten thousand acres. It was a part of the grant to Col. James Patton from the crown of England.

Gen. and Mrs. Preston urged Mrs. Russell to take a house in Abingdon, where she could be near them and their children. There they could see her every day, and take care of her; and there she would have such church privileges as the village offered. There, too, she would more frequently meet, and could entertain more comfortably, the Methodist preachers. These and other considerations were especially urged by William C. Preston, who was devoted to his grandmother, and with whom he was a great favorite and pet.

The house which Gen. Preston had built opposite the court-house was burned just as it was finished and partly furnished, and he was obliged to crowd his family into a small house which stood where he resided until 1836. He bought the lots in rear of it to Valley street, then known as "the back street."

Mrs. Russell yielded to the solicitations of her grandson, and authorized him to rent a house for her. He did so promptly, and congratulated himself on securing the commodious and comfortable frame house which stood near the site of Mr. D. G. Thomas's brick house. It could be reached by the family of Gen. Preston through the garden, and without the exposure of going upon Main street. With great glee Wm. C. Preston told his grandmother what he had done, and expatiated upon the advantages of the position, and how happy all the children would be at having her so near them, and so nicely and quietly fixed on the "back street." She listened with interest and apparent pleasure to his animated description until he pronounced the last two words. Then her expression changed, and, after a pause, she asked, "Where did you say the house is?" "On the back street," he replied. The old lady drew herself up, and with the air of offended dignity said: "Why, William! would you put *your* grandmother on the *back street*? No, sir; I am not proud, but I will not live in a house on the *back street of Abingdon!*" This settled the question, and Mr. Preston canceled the lease. Gen. and Mrs. Preston offered to rent or purchase any other house that could be had in the village if she would consent to live there; but she refused, because she preferred the quiet of the country. She would not live with either of her daughters. Finally she decided to take the log-house which stood near the creek, above and in sight of the "Town House," where her daughter, Mrs. Thompson, lived. This house is no longer standing. It was a story and a half high, with two rooms below and two above. One of the lower rooms was quite large, and was used by Mrs. Russell both as a bed-room and sitting-room. The other, though much smaller, was large enough in those primitive times to accommodate old Father George Eiken, his wife, and two children; and there they lived for several years. Before and after they occupied it, it was kept as the "prophet's chamber," and ever ready for any preacher or circuit-rider who wished to rest a day or more at this hallowed Bethel. There was a smaller log-cabin in the yard where single men could sleep. The kitchen and servants' house were separate from but quite near the dwelling. The stable was large enough for several horses. In the large room on the first floor of the dwelling-house was the movable pulpit, so often referred to by visitors. Every minister who came there was asked to use it, whenever a few of the neighbors could be collected for religious services. In the room above there were stored every autumn boxes of walnuts, hickory-nuts, filberts, and barrels of apples. It was the children's privilege to bring these down, and then, grouping themselves near "grandma's" feet, would crack the nuts on a piece of rough iron put upon the hearth with a hammer she kept for that purpose.

Mrs. Russell was above the medium height. She was about five feet seven inches, and in the prime of life must have been of imposing presence. She may not have been what would be called "a beautiful woman," but no face with such brow and eyes could have been plain or unattractive. Hers was one of those faces which had the charm of being more pleasant the more familiar it became. In the eyes of her grandchildren she was a beautiful old lady. Her eyes were of a soft, grayish blue, which varied in color under different lights, and changed with the emotions of her mind and heart: when she looked at her grandchildren, or those she especially loved, they had a sweet, tender expression that touched the heart with a pleasure like the soft breath of summer evening, and drew the little ones by magnetic power toward her to be petted and caressed; in conversation, they expressed every phase of feeling, and twinkled with fun, gleamed with animation, or sparkled when earnest and vivid thoughts agitated her mind. Both in intellect and person she resembled her brother, Patrick Henry. She had the same fertile and vivid imagination, the same ready command of language and aptness of illustration, and the same flexibility of voice and grace of elocution. These attributes made her narrations of incidents and descriptions of scenes and characters not only graphic, but fascinating; and when roused to their full power in prayer, they rose to an eloquence that thrilled or awed the soul. Her every-day dress was very plain, but neat. Except in warm weather, when she wore dark calico, her gown was of some gray material resembling flannel (called, I believe, "bath-coating"), made simply, and reaching to the tops of her shoes. Around her neck was a cambric handkerchief, crossed over the chest and fastened at the waist. Sometimes this handkerchief was of soft material, full and puffed. A small, plain cap, with a narrow, fluted frill,

completed her toilet. On Sundays, when she went to
church, or on ceremonial occasions, she wore a black silk
dress, more elaborately made, an old-fashioned bonnet of
the best material, and such wrappings as the season required. She never kept a carriage, and always mounted
her horse from a big stump in the yard, some three feet in
diameter, reached by steps of solid blocks of wood. Sometimes she presented a queer appearance when she stuck on
her head a man's low-crowned felt hat, and walked about
the yard and garden. And yet such was the simple dignity
of her bearing that nothing she did seemed incongruous or
ridiculous. Her impetuosity and impatience would have
been so in any other, but with her they were natural, and
scarcely provoked a smile. These traits were often manifested in the messages and dispatches sent to the Salt-works,
six miles from her house. There she had an unlimited letter of credit for any thing she wanted, and from there she
drew her money and supplies.

It not unfrequently occurred that an unlooked-for number of visitors came to the house, and for each person there
was a horse, and occasionally a servant. No one was ever
turned away; all were sure of a hearty welcome. She
stowed her guests away as the Methodists divide their con-
gregations—the women and children were put in one room,
and the men and boys in another. Then there was scur-
rying around for supplies, and Mrs. Russell's peculiarities
were brought into the clearest light. She would stand upon
the door-step, and, in that clear voice that sounded like a
softened bugle-note, call for her servant "Dick;" and by the
time he presented himself she would scribble a note to the
manager at the Salt-works, and *pinning* it to the lapel of
his coat would say: "Now, Dick, run and saddle the horse,
and fly over to the Salt-works; be in a hurry! don't stop!
and bring me some meal"—or meat, or money, or whatever
else the emergency required. It was necessary to *tell* Dick
the message, for those hasty notes were often in such hiero-
glyphics that none but the initiated could decipher them.

Dick (called by the negroes Blue Dick) was a remarkable person in appearance and character—a perfect Albino, though of pure African blood. He had the coarse features of his race, but the dull white color seen in some of the lower grades of Circassians. His head was covered by a full suit of creamy-white hair that looked like a big mop. His eyelashes and eyebrows were white, and his eyes had a slight pinkish tinge, and were crossed, and called "dancing eyes," because of their nervous restlessness. As the light of the sun affected them painfully, he habitually kept the lids partially closed, and with his head a little bent on one side he looked askant at those who spoke to him. His uncertain vision and dancing eyes communicated a shaking motion to his head; and as he stood uncovered in the attitude of respect before his mistress, his mass of hair, though carefully combed, puffed out over his head and shook as if stirred by a gentle breeze. His sight was better in cloudy days and at night. Like most of his race, he was a fearless rider, and on those hasty trips to the Salt-works dashed over the mountain and through the steep gorges of the hills at a pace that the boldest of horsemen would hesitate to follow. His intellect was feeble, but his heart was like Nathanael's —free of guile, and full of the gentlest and kindest feelings. Left an orphan at an early age, he was taken to "the house" by Mrs. Russell and brought up under her immediate care. To her his attachment and devotion were boundless. While quite a youth he was converted, and joined the Methodist Church, and lived and died as pure, consistent, and earnest a Christian as can be found in any sphere of life. After Mrs. Russell's death, he was taken to Abingdon, and was cared for by Gen. Preston's family, with whom he lived. Dick imbibed the spirit and followed the example of his "old mistress" in praying. There was no occasion and no place when and where, if the Spirit moved him, he would not kneel down and pray. As he was oblivious of his surroundings in his rapt devotions, he gave distinct utterance to his petitions. Often transported by his emotions, his voice rose to a pitch that could be heard all over the premises. He held prayer-meetings for the other servants, and was indefatigable in urging upon the young to get aboard the "old ship of Zion" before she sailed for the kingdom and they were left on the shore to perish. He lived to a good old age, and then sunk to rest as a child drops to sleep, in the confidence of a reasonable and religious hope, and in unshaken faith of a glorious resurrection and life with Jesus in heaven.

I am induced to give this notice of Dick because I regard him as a striking illustration of the transforming and elevating power of the Christian religion, and of its thorough adaptation to the wants of the soul in every condition of life and every grade of intellect. In Dick we have a poor, half-witted African slave, who from physical defects could not be taught to read, and yet who had as distinct a realization of the atonement of Christ, and of pardon of sin and acceptance with God through Christ, as the most profound theologian, and who exhibited, by a humble, consistent, religious life, the power of faith in a crucified Saviour.

As soon as the horses of the guests were disposed of— "hitched" to the rack or fence if they were to stay for a few hours, or taken to the stable if to remain longer—and all were assembled in the "big room," Mrs. Russell would say: "Now, let us unite in prayer." If a minister or class-leader were present, the pulpit was placed in position, and "the brother" was requested to read a portion of Scripture and lead in prayer. If neither of those Church officials were of the guests, she herself led in prayer; and to hear her was a privilege that none ever enjoyed and forgot. Often there was a simplicity in the personality of her petitions that was as appropriate as touching, and made the persons prayed for feel as though they were borne in her strong arms of love immediately before the throne of grace. On other occasions, when her feelings were aroused by joy or sorrow or religious excitement, she would touch the whole gamut of human emotions and hush the soul into profound adoration, as if in the presence of God, or melt to tears of contrition or gratitude all who were present. Every incident in life was an occasion for prayer. The joy of meeting, the pain of parting, thankfulness for blessings or mercies, submission under privations, disappointments, or bereavements, were alike to be carried to God in prayer. So large a portion of her time was passed upon her knees that the skin became indurated and callous. She did not, however, confine herself to the daylight and to kneeling, but often during the night would continue her devotions in subdued tones. Her little granddaughters, when visiting her, soon understood the sounds that roused them, and learned to control every sign that would interrupt her. To give vitality to her prayers for her immediate family, the old lady seized the opportunities afforded by their visits to drop into their young minds the precious seeds of religious truth. And who can tell how much of the earnest piety and rare usefulness which characterized the lives of those granddaughters was due to the early lessons of that devoted woman?

No matter who the visitor might be, the prayer was not omitted. A member of the family relates the following story.

When Mr. Madison was a candidate for the presidency in 1808, he made a visit to Gen. Preston at the Salt-works. His wife, the celebrated Dolly Payne, was a kinswoman of Mrs. Russell, and Mr. Madison himself was also allied to the family, and drawn more closely to it by the marriage of Col. Thomas Madison to a sister of Mrs. Russell, and his guardianship of her daughter who had married Gen. Francis Preston.

Mr. Madison was not so engrossed by his presidential canvass as to be unmindful of these social claims. Accompanied by Gen. Preston, he sought Mrs. Russell at her own home. She received him at the door with a cordial welcome; and as soon as he was fairly in the house, entirely undismayed by the dignity of her visitor, she pursued her usual habit; and being a tall woman, and he a short man, she laid her

2

hand upon his head, and gently pressing him to his knees, as she knelt by his side, with all her force and zeal she prayed for him as the prospective head of the nation.

Speaking of this occurrence afterward, Mr. Madison is reported as saying: "I have heard all the first orators of America, but I never heard any eloquence as great as that prayer of Mrs. Russell on the occasion of my visit to her."

She did not pray in church, nor in large assemblies. Her meek and gentle nature shrunk from notoriety, and she kept strictly within the sphere of what she believed was woman's true position.

When Wm. C. Preston was expected on his return from Europe, Mrs. Russell was at Gen. Preston's. He had been absent more than a year, and she, with the family, was anxiously awaiting his arrival. As soon as the rapture of greetings was over, and she had pressed him to her heart and kissed him again and again, she said: "Now, let us all unite in prayer, and return thanks to God for bringing safely back to us our dear son." Wm. C. Preston frequently recurred to this incident, and rarely without adding that he never heard such an eloquent effusion of pious gratitude. The family were moved to tears, and wept from excess of joy. And yet one of the reasons for thankfulness she especially emphasized was that God had shielded him from "the wiles of those wicked foreign women," and brought him back "unencumbered by a frivolous French wife."

This brief and imperfect sketch may give some idea of the woman who for nearly forty years was a zealous Methodist and conscientious Christian. All of her influence "in the sphere of life where God had placed her" was used in promoting true religion, and in aiding to establish on a firm foundation the Church of her choice—"Jesus Christ himself being the chief corner-stone." She was brought up in the faith of the Protestant Episcopal Church, but was not confirmed, as there was no bishop then in Virginia to administer this rite. The fervor and zeal of the early frontier Methodists were congenial to her impulsive and enthusiastic nature, and she entered with all the ardor of that gifted nature into their feelings and purposes. She took a deep interest in and felt a cordial sympathy for that class of toiling, self-sacrificing circuit-riders, the true pioneers of religion, who fearlessly sought the "lost sheep" on the outskirts of society and in the sequestered gorges of the mountains, and brought them back to the fold of God. Her house was always a shelter for them in the times of their brief repose; and thither they came, and drew from that perennial fountain of piety fresh courage and vigor for their noble work. Her peculiar gifts of conversation and exhortation were exerted in elevating their tone of feeling, softening, and polishing their manners, and indicating courses of reading. Many of them were rough, uneducated mountaineers, full of zeal and purpose, but without the refinement and polish which result from associating with women of cultivation and experience. Nor did they go away from her hospitable home empty-handed. A new suit of clothes, a fresh horse, or money for necessary expenses, were bestowed with a tact that never offended the most delicate sensibilities. The recipient doubtless often felt that those gifts were more for the cause in which he was engaged than for himself. Richly did she deserve the title of "mother in Israel." To this day, after the lapse of two generations, her spirit seems to hover over the region where most of her life was spent, and in that community many devout Methodists are illustrating by their walk and conversation "the beauty of holiness."

In those pioneer days of Methodism in South-west Virginia converts were chiefly made among the poor and lowly. They therefore felt that in winning the wide social influence of this gifted woman they were not only advancing their denominational interests, but, what was far more important to them, promoting the cause of true religion. They cherished her greatly, and have embalmed her memory in the heart and the traditions and the history of their noble Church. They have gone still farther, and sent it down to posterity by a permanent memorial of the most complimentary kind. The earliest educational venture of their denomination in that quarter of the State (Emory and Henry College) bears united the name of this devoted woman and that of one of their most esteemed bishops.

Of Mrs. Russell's adult descendants there are very few who are not members of one or another of the evangelical Churches. God's promises never fail; and if the sainted dead are permitted to see fruit of their travail on earth, how the soul of that "mother in Israel" must rejoice as she welcomes her children, one after another, into the rest prepared for the children of God!

"Mrs. Elizabeth Russell departed this life the 18th day of March, 1825. She lay five weeks and three days of an illness caused by a fall. She met death with Christian composure, after living an exemplary life of seventy-six years, and was buried, by her request, at Aspenvale."

This is the record left us by her granddaughter, Mrs. Maria McAnally, who was the companion and nurse of Mrs. Russell for several years before her death. After her death, when Dr. Wm. P. Thompson decided to move to Missouri, Mrs. Sarah B. Preston insisted that he should leave his daughters (her nieces) with her, and not expose them to the rough, unprotected life of the frontier whither he was going. To this he assented, and Eliza and Maria Thompson were regarded as children of Mrs. Preston's family from that time.

Eliza married Mr. Williams, of Tennessee, who died not long afterward. His wife sunk under the blow, and soon followed him to the grave.

Maria married the Rev. D. R. McAnally, a distinguished Methodist minister, now residing in St. Louis, Mo.

Both of these ladies were remarkable for their consistent religious lives, and their devotion to the Church of the grandmother who had nourished them in purity and holiness from infancy. Mrs. Williams left no children. Only a son and daughter of Mrs. McAnally survive. The former is a

Methodist minister, and upon the latter the mantle of her sainted mother seems to have fallen.

A graceful and appropriate tribute to Mrs. Russell's character was paid by the Hon. Charles C. Johnstone in an obituary published in the Abingdon *Gazette;* but the files of that paper, with many valuable public and private papers, were destroyed when Abingdon was burned in 1863, and no copy of it is now known to exist.   THOS. L. PRESTON.

University of Virginia, April, 1887.

❧❦APPENDIX.❦❧

MRS. ELIZABETH RUSSELL.

FROM "SIXTY YEARS IN A SCHOOL-ROOM." BY MRS. JULIA A. TEVIS.

ABOUT this time I became acquainted with this excellent but eccentric old lady, Mrs. Russell, through the medium of General Frank Preston's family. Mrs. Russell's first husband was General William Campbell, the hero of King's Mountain. Mrs. Preston was the only child of this marriage. . . .

Mrs. Russell was in every way an extraordinary woman. The sister of Patrick Henry, she possessed some of his characteristics. Her second husband, General Russell, was quite as distinguished as the first for worth and bravery. Both she and General Russell were faithful members of the Methodist Church. They were converted in the good old-fashioned way, when nobody objected to shouting if it came from an overflowing heart filled with the love of God. The old General walked worthy of his vocation until he was taken home to a better world, leaving his excellent widow a true type of Wesleyan Methodism. "Madame Russell," as she was generally called, was a "mother in Israel," and the Methodist preachers in those days esteemed her next to Bishop Asbury. . . . At this place (near the camp-ground in the vicinity of the Sulphur Springs) a wooden house had been erected under her special supervision and according to her own idea of consistency. Here she lived like the good old Moravian, Count Zinzendorf, who wrote over the portals of his mansion:

> " As guests we only here remain,
> And hence the house is slight and plain
>   (*Therefore, turn to the stronghold, ye prisoners of hope*);
> We have a better home above,
> And there we find our warmest love."

There were two rooms below, large and spacious, the one first entered being her common sitting-room. A door from this opened into one much larger, which contained a pulpit and seats for a moderate-sized congregation. When a preacher visited her she said: " Brother, how long will you tarry? There's the pulpit; shall I send out and call together a congregation?" No visitors came to see her and remained an hour without being asked to pray. If they declined she herself prayed, mentioning by name every person for whom she prayed.

She dressed in the style of '76—full skirts, with an over-garment, long, flowing, open in front, and confined at the waist by a girdle, and made of a material called Bath coating. In this girdle were tucked two or three pocket-handkerchiefs. The sleeves of her dress came just below her elbows, the lower part of the arms being covered with long, half-handed gloves. She wore a kerchief of linen lawn, white as snow, and sometimes an apron of the same material; and on her head a very plain cap, above which was usually placed a broad-brimmed hat given her by Bishop Asbury in days long gone by, and worn by the old lady with probably the same feeling that Elisha wore Elijah's mantle. She was erect as in the meridian of life, though she must have been seventy years old when I first saw her. A magnificent-looking woman, "she walked every inch a queen," reminding me of one of the old-fashioned pictures of Vandyke. She never shook the hand of a poor Methodist preacher in parting without leaving in it a liberal donation; she knew that the gospel was free, but she also knew that "the laborer was worthy of his hire." The celebrated William C. Preston, of South Carolina, her oldest grandson, loved her with a devotion highly commendable to himself and agreeable to his grandmother. In his yearly visits to his native home his carriage was found first at the door of her humble dwelling. He gave evidence on his dying-bed that his grandmother's religion had been his guiding star, and his love for her shone as brightly in the evening as in the morning and meridian of his life. I knew William C. Preston well. He was distinguished as a man of cultivated intellect, sound judgment, and warm affections. As an orator I do not think he ever had his superior in the United States, though he sought not the world-wide celebrity he might have attained. He was heard to say, while President of Columbia College, in South Carolina: "I believe teaching is my vocation, and I would that I had spent my whole life in striving, like Socrates, to educate the young, for I have proved the difficulty of instructing those more advanced in life."

An anecdote related to me by Mrs. Russell illustrates the estimation in which Patrick Henry was held throughout his native State. When she first came to South-western Virginia she attended a camp-meeting, where her relationship to Patrick Henry became whispered about. Such was the crowd that immediately pressed around her, to get a glimpse of one so distinguished, that she was only rescued from being crushed by the surrounding multitude by mounting upon a stump, where she was compelled to turn round and round, amidst the uproarious demonstrations of an enthusiastic people, who cried out, "Hurrah for Patrick Henry!" with an occasional shout for General Campbell.

EMENDATIONS BY THE AUTHOR.

[Note to page 23; lines 20-29.]

This was written before I read "The Life of Patrick Henry," by Moses Coit Tyler. He proves that Mr. Henry was baptized and made a member of the Protestant Episcopal Church in early life, and that he lived and died an exemplary member of it, and communed as often as an opportunity was offered. On such occasions he always fasted until he had communicated, and spent the day in the greatest retirement. This he did both while Governor and afterward. (Tyler's Life of Henry, pp. 349-350.) The influences deduced from his character and the tenor of his life are confirmed and established by conclusive evidence.

[Note to page 31; to follow line 20.]

William C. Preston so strikingly resembled his grandfather, General William Campbell, that on one occasion his life was endangered by it. He was traveling from Abingdon, Va., to Columbia, S. C., on horseback alone. The route he followed was very much the same as that taken by the expedition led by General Campbell which culminated in the battle of King's Mountain. When he reached the vicinity of the battle-field he stopped about midday at a house to rest, get dinner, and have his horse fed. While waiting until dinner was ready he lay down upon a rough bench in the porch, and was nearly asleep when he was awakened by the presence of an old woman staring at him with a fiendish expression. As he aroused himself she retired into the house. This excited his apprehension, and deciding to test the matter further, he relapsed into his former position and feigned being asleep. Soon the old woman reappeared, and, bending over him, scrutinized more closely his features, her own darkened by intense and concentrated passion. This time, more thoroughly aroused, he met her gaze, and as she did so she said, "Young man, what is your name?" He answered, "My name is Preston." "Where are you from, and where are you going?" she fiercely demanded. "I am from Virginia, and am going to Columbia, S. C.," he calmly replied. "Well," said she, "I am glad your name is not Campbell. If it *was*, you wouldn't get out of these mountains alive, for you are the very image of the worst man I ever saw, one General William Campbell. Get up now; your dinner is ready." Mr. Preston dispatched his dinner quickly, carefully suppressed his Christian name, left promptly, and made good speed from that neighborhood during the afternoon. He subsequently ascertained that this woman was the widow of a notorious Tory who was hanged after the battle of King's Mountain.